CONTENTS

C000069753

About the Author
New Non-Fiction By Laura Mariani   vi
Also By Laura Mariani   vii

A NEW YORK ADVENTURE

Quote   5
A New York Adventure   7

SEARCHING FOR GOREN

Preface   39
Searching For Goren   41
Afterword   53

TASTING FREEDOM

Preface   59
Tasting Freedom   61
Quote   69
Afterword   71
Disclaimer   72
Author's Note   73

THE NINE LIVES OF GABRIELLE: FOR THREE, SHE PLAYS

BOOK 1-3 COLLECTION

LAURA MARIANI

The PEOPLE ALCHEMIST

ABOUT THE AUTHOR

Laura Mariani is an Author, Speaker and Entrepreneur.

She started her consulting business after a successful career as Senior HR Director within global brands in FMCG, Retail, Media and Pharma.

Laura is incredibly passionate about helping other women to break through barriers limiting their personal and/or professional fulfilment. Her best selling nonfiction *STOP IT! It is all in your head* and the *THINK, LOOK & ACT THE PART* series have been described as success and transformation 101.

She is a Fellow of the Chartered Institute of Personnel & Development (FCIPD), Fellow of the Australian Human Resources Institute (FAHRI), Fellow of the Institute of Leadership & Management (FInstLM), Member of the Society of Human Resources Management (SHRM) and Member of the Change Institute.

She is based in London, England with a strong penchant for travel and visiting new places. She is a food lover, ballet fanatic, passionate about music, art, theatre. She likes painting and drawing (for self-expression not selling but hey, you never know...), tennis, rugby, and of course fashion (the Pope is Catholic after all).

NEW NON-FICTION BY LAURA MARIANI

ALSO BY LAURA MARIANI

Non-Fiction

STOP IT! It is all in your head

The RULE BOOK to Smash The infamous glass ceiling - For women & young women everywhere - personal transformation & success 101.

The Think, Look & Act The Part Series.

Think The Part

Upgrade your consciousness and mind-set. Make winning a key part of your life and business.

Look The Part

Upgrade your personal brand. Make presenting your unique Best Self a key part of your life and business.

Act The Part

A personal coach to act in spite of fear, right here, right now.

More non-fiction books and courses are coming soon. For new releases, giveaways and pre-release specials check www. thepeoplealchemist.com

You can also buy my books and courses directly from me at www. payhip.com / LauraMariani

ThePeopleAlchemist Press publishes self help, inspirational and transformational books, resources and products to help #TheWomanAlchemist in every woman to change her life/career and transmute any circumstance into gold, a bit like magic to **Unlock Ignite Transform.**

ISBN: 978-1-915501-00-4

A NEW YORK ADVENTURE

THE NINE LIVES OF GABRIELLE: FOR
THREE SHE PLAYS - BOOK 1

To New York, one of my three loves

"YOU'RE ONLY HERE NOW;
YOU'RE ONLY ALIVE IN THIS MOMENT"
- **JON KABAT-ZINN**

G abrielle was getting ready to go out.
A surprise from Mr Wonderful.

Out for dinner and then to the Opera. Going out again felt incredible after almost two years of off and on lockdowns. They were celebrating the day that they met. He was always full of surprises: spontaneous, romantic and thoughtful.

She hadn't had the time to think carefully about what to wear and was getting ready at the last minute. She decided on wearing the same dress she wore when they met: the white dress culpable for so many mischiefs, the dress that started it all.

Albeit it was so lovely to go out again now that all the restrictions had been lifted, it was also so strange seeing a mix-match of people with and without masks everywhere you went. The anxiety and slight fear when hearing someone coughing. You can just see the suspicion on people's faces. "Has he/she got IT?" The new dreaded C-word.

However, slowly and surely, life is getting back to normality. Time is passing by, and life needs to go on. She missed travelling and going out. Socialising and the theatre, she loved the theatre, and Mr Wonderful knew her well.

BANG! Ouch...

The collision was surprisingly strong, considering they were both just walking. Gabrielle had lost her balance, but he was quick and promptly grabbed her by the waist to keep her from falling. Unfortunately, her coffee wasn't that lucky and splattered everywhere.

. . .

E-V-E-R-Y-W-H-E-R-E on her white dress.

Memories. The smell of coffee and cologne. He smelled real good. Affirmations were still playing in her ears when they banged into each other.

"I am a Goddess; I am a Queen"
   - very empowering, perhaps a tad scary for a man to hear when they first meet you.

"I am so so sorry," he said.

"Gosh, thank you, Jesus, he is so handsome,"
   Gabrielle thought as she looked up at the piercing blue eyes, the dazzling smile peaking through the mask now half down his chin.

Gabrielle felts like he was looking straight into her soul. He was genuinely mortified by what had happened.

"I'm OK, thank you. Not a big deal, really. It is only coffee," she said, playing it cool.

He didn't stop looking straight into her eyes, not even for a second. She didn't know if to back up to keep some parvence of social distancing (and decor) or hold the stare. Fuck it. Hold it.

She felt like getting closer instead. She didn't. He offered to get her dress dry-cleaned for her. Gabrielle wondered if he was living in London or if he got stuck here when lockdown started. He had that distinctive North American, New York accent.

"Please, let me do this for you. I live just around the corner: if the dry-cleaners are closed, I can wash your dress and have it ready in a couple of hours. Perhaps even make you a coffee while you wait. One that you can drink this time,"
    he insisted.

"Wait, did he just ask me back to his place and offer to wash my dress?" pondering,
    "This is the type of exchange you see in Hallmark movies. Or the real crime police dramas".

She squinted with her deep dark eyes staring into his and said:

"Is this a cheap ploy to see me naked?"

"No, no, no, YES "
    ... mortified
    "No, no. I mean would be great but no".

        • • •

She smiled profusely and felt like teasing him.

"I feel like I'm in a scene from the Vicar of Dibley: where is the camera?"

"What?"

looking puzzled and obviously not getting the reference.

"Sorry, British cultural reference. I'm kidding. I'm OK, seriously, no need to go through that much trouble. It is only coffee".

And then he asked her for a date. Gabrielle remembered how she quickly glanced at his hands to see if there was any appearance of a wedding ring. Both hands, to be sure. And no, there was no ring or any signs that he was wearing one regularly either.

He offered to cook too.

"What about social distancing?"

Gabrielle said.

"I think we broke that rule already. We can eat outside if that makes you feel any better or safer,"

he said.

"I don't know you".

"I'm trying to remedy that",

and sensing her reluctance
"Can I have at least your number?"

Gabrielle was intrigued and attracted to him, so she gave him her number. He had just finished tapping her number into his mobile when her phone started ringing in her pocket.

"Are you going to get that?" He asked.

"Pardon?"

"Your phone, are you going to answer it?"

"No, it's rude; I am talking to you. I can see who called me later".

"It's me".

"You can't be missing me already; I'm still here,"
    Gabrielle said (he is keen, a good sign).

"I just want to make sure I have the right number. And you now have mine too"
    he was grinning too.
    "Are you sure I cannot convince you to have dinner with me tonight?"

· · ·

"Not tonight".

"Another night then. Tomorrow?"

He was sure of himself without being arrogant and persistent. He knew exactly what he wanted and was going for it.

Gabrielle felt really good about the encounter and excited as she hadn't been for a long time. She remembered waving and walking away. Actually, she had never felt like this before. Her body was on fire, her spirit soaring, and she was walking on clouds.

It would have been the perfect exit had she not turned around to see if he was still there. But she couldn't help herself. She had to.

He was still there, standing still, looking. Smiling.

As she turned around the corner, her phone vibrated, a text:

"Now, I am missing you."
  "that's understandable", she replied.

Just like that, that day, everything changed. He was everything she always wanted but wasn't quite ready for before. And it was still going.

· · ·

"Honey, are you almost ready?"
Mr Wonderful asked, peeking through the bedroom door,
"the Uber will be here in the next few minutes".

"Where are we going exactly now?"
as it was too early for the Opera.

"Dinner".

"I know, you said. Where though?"
Gabrielle, the in-control planner, needed to know.

"I made a reservation for Balthazar in Covent Garden".
Nice, and walking distance to the Royal Opera House. She
had mentioned to him that she had been in New York; he
must have remembered.

Balthazar was busy. Very.

They were greeted as the walked in and taken straight to their
table. The relatively small room, with faux-nicotine-stained
walls, a station clock, and the poised amber hue, is almost
made for Instagram.
There was a lively buzz in the air.

Just as well, Mr Wonderful had made a reservation because
there was a queue outside waiting to be seated, and many
who tried a walk-in turned away, disappointed with the wait.

. . .

Gabrielle ordered the mussels for the starter and steak tartare for the main course. Mr Wonderful had ordered champagne seemingly on tap to wash everything down.

He was soo good at remembering all the little details and celebrating every occasion, no matter how small or big. Anything she ever said, he listened and acted upon. She was speechless actually that he remembered so much about everything that she told him.

He was spontaneous, romantic, thoughtful, and passionate with piercing blue eyes. No wonder she called him Mr Wonderful.

They were seated in the right-hand corner of the restaurant, just in front of the bar with a good view of the room and the window, great for people-watching, should you want to.

They could barely hear each other lost amongst the live jazz, the chitchat and the noise of plates and cutlery, but, at the same time, it was very intimate and cosy. Even in the middle of a crowd, Mr Wonderful only had eyes for her.

Chitchat, chitchat.

The same sounds, different vibe.

Clink clink … clink …

· · ·

Gabrielle adored grand set-piece spectacular restaurants with ambience, and Balthazar is undoubtedly that and perhaps, one of the best brasseries in London for its atmosphere, happy, friendly staff and service, living up to the reputation of his New York City original.

The first time she had visited Balthazar in New York was on the weekend for brunch, steak and eggs, New York pancakes and Balthazar Bloody Mary.

The VP took her there. They had only just met a few days earlier.

skahdeedath bideedoodop… gahdugat …

"NYC Balthazar is much bigger than this one", was going through her head.

It was in the midst of the full Sex and The City hype at that time. A place everyone wanted to be seen at.

And the VP made sure they had the most visible table in the room.

He was waving at people, smiling.

"You see that man on the corner?"

Gabrielle turned her head slightly to see what he was talking about.

· · ·

"He is the CEO of such and such …. Major client".

"That one over there is the anchor of NBC News",
name dropping
"and that blonde woman over there is in a famous soap opera".

People watching. Or, even more important, been watched. They were seated bang in the middle of the room, which was definitely good for that. Not a great table to have a conversation and get to know someone.

Then again, Gabrielle didn't think that's why they were there.

That was the first date with the VP after Gabrielle arrived in New York.

The trip was a last-minute decision after a long-term relationship break-up.

Another failed relationship.

Gabrielle had reached boiling point and felt claustrophobic. She needed to escape, an adventure, re-group and re-think what she would do. She felt like she had thrown five years down the drain. She had given everything she could and had nothing more to offer right now.

"Let's get married and have babies,"

he said out of the blue, after five years and all the previous talk about a commitment that went nowhere.

Unbelievable. Too little, too late.

Mentally she had moved on. She wasn't sure anymore if she saw a future with him. Growing old with him. Or as the father of her children.

Her friends always told her,

"Why don't you get pregnant?
    You know, a-c-c-i-d-e-n-t-a-l-l-y. Things happen all the time, and you'll at least have a child".

Gabrielle knew that some (many? few?) women do that, and sometimes it works well. Sometimes not so much.
    But she, she could never bring herself to do it. To even try.

There are enough unwanted children in the world, and bringing another potential unwanted one in didn't feel like an option to her. Although to be fair, she was always planning for her career, move after move, and it never quite seemed to be the right time to get pregnant.
    Moving town, travelling, and a new bigger job always sounded more like desirable and viable options.

Perhaps she didn't want a child.

The idea of a child, yes. The idea of being a mother, yes.

Doing it not so much. She had thought if having children was so ingrained that she had to want it, being a mother as the pinnacle of being a woman. She always wanted to be free.

Always wanted to travel, free to do what she wanted, when she wanted.

Marriage too.

The idea of an all-encompassing, consuming, can't live without someone love affair was thrilling. A strong man to look after her. Finding a man she could bear 24/7 without feeling trapped, not so much. And now, all she wanted was to take off.

Just go somewhere.

New York - the Big Apple dream - had always been lurking in the background. This was the perfect opportunity to take the plunge. So she wrote to her boss requesting time off and got her tickets. Three months in New York, a mini-sabbatical. Longer than a holiday but short enough not to need a working visa.

On her taxi ride to the airport, she felt like Indiana Jones

(ok, mini Indiana Jones); it was her first-ever trip alone, non-work-related.

Not visiting anybody. Nothing planned. Just her and New York.

Exhilarating and scary AF.

The flight felt much longer than she imagined, maybe because she had to squeeze between two enormous individuals overflowing into her seat. Perhaps because they never stopped moving, talking, eating. ALL the way throughout the flight.

"Jesus, what's wrong with actually keeping quiet for a few hours. Or just sleep",
    she asked herself, already knowing the answer. To Gabrielle, it felt like people are afraid of silence, and they need desperately to fill in.

"God knows what they are afraid will happen if they are alone with their thoughts. So most of the time, people fill the void with absolute total nonsense. And unfortunately, on a plane, there isn't much of an escape route. You have to listen. Well, kind of".

Chitchat, chitchat, blah blah blah…

And constant eating.

"Really? Who brings snacks on a long haul flight? I'm sure starvation will not sneak up on you if you don't constantly munch on something. Out loud. The airline already provides food, starvation prevented".

Note to self: MUST book business class for the return flight.

As the plane landed at JFK, people proceeded calmly out of the aircraft, following the different signs directing toward

Customs and Border Protection. Brits are good at queuing, and it comes naturally. Whilst the passengers were arriving near the actual desks, Gabrielle was jilted out of her thoughts:

"Ma'am, step behind the yellow line".

"Is she talking to me?"
Gabrielle thought. "Did she just call me Ma'am?"

She didn't know if she was more upset about being called Ma'am ("do I look that old?"), especially as the officer didn't look that much younger herself or being shouted at by an overbearing sturdy officer WITH A GUN.

Apparently, she was doing something wrong. Gabrielle didn't know what it was, but it seemed to have annoyed her. A lot.
The Border Protection officer got closer to Gabrielle, far too close for comfort because she was sure they weren't about to *faire la bise* and proceeded to shout, again, explaining
("I must have looked really tick", she wondered),

"Ma'am, step behind the yellow line. You have not been admitted into the United States until you have gone through my colleague at the desk. Step behind the yellow line."

"What? Really? I'm pretty sure the plane landed at JFK, and I'm pretty sure JFK happens to be in the US of A. So what is she going to do? Throw me back into the sea?"

· · ·

As all these thoughts were going through her mind, Gabrielle sheepishly said,

" Sure, no problem, officer"

she didn't feel that courageous to argue with an armed, angry person in authority.

The reputation of trigger-happy American police (whatever) is infamous and, unfortunately, or fortunately, was imprinted in her mind. She also had images of being locked up with no contact with the external world and sent back. Or kept somewhere.

God knows where.

"I have watched too many police movies,"
Gabrielle thought.

What a contrast from the officer behind the desk.

He was a young male in his late twenties or early thirties, seemingly shy. And he was unlucky enough to have three ladies who had just landed from Manchester at his desk. They were having a great time, which seemed to have started on their plane, or before, with copious alcohol. One might say they were "tipsy".

And determined to have a good time.

New York was their stop for the night before embarking on a Caribbean cruise, and they were officially on holiday, probably FROM Manchester. They must have been in their late fifties, early sixties, or at least what looked like sixty or thereabout in Gabrielle's mind. They were making all sorts of advances to the poor guy who, by now, had become red-faced up to his roots.

And was getting redder by the minute.

They were totally shameless, and who can blame them? He was cute, wearing a uniform (always helps) and reinforced by each other and vodka martinis.

He couldn't wait to get them off his desk soon enough.

Bless.

Then came her turn. Gabrielle was sure she had never been asked that many questions going through any other customs in any other country. At least she couldn't remember. Neither did she think they sounded like legitimate questions (to grant entry into the country).

Perhaps he was reasserting his authority and regaining control after the cruise ladies, or maybe that's what he usually asked. Who knows.

Gabrielle preferred to think there was some mild flirtation going on. But, hey, he was cute, and it was a friendly welcome to New York. She felt smug and almost tempted to turn back and poke her tongue out at the

"Step behind the yellow line" officer but thought perhaps better not.

. . .

She stepped out of the airport and looked for the taxi lane.

"324 West 44th Street, please. The TownePlace Suite Manhattan, please"
let the adventure begin.

As they were driving toward the city, the taxi driver made small talk. Gabrielle was distracted: she was soaking in the atmosphere, excited about what the next three months would bring.

She had chosen an extended-stay boutique-style hotel right in the heartbeat of NYC's Times Square and within walking distance to Broadway, Restaurant Row, Macy's Herald Square, Empire State Building and many other famous attractions.
She wanted to have the most authentic experience possible in a neighbourhood-style accommodation with a kitchenette.

Of course, New York is full of places to eat everywhere, and she could easily go out for dinner if she wanted to. However, she both liked the convenience and pretending she was living there, if only for a little bit.
Perhaps cook a few meals from time to time.

Come to think of it, Gabrielle had never been out for dinner or in a pub by herself.

. . .

E-V-E-R.

Even when meeting people, she always checked to ensure they arrived first.

"Baby steps Gabri, baby steps,"
    she said to herself.

She flew in early in the morning to enjoy almost a full first day and then crash at "normal" sleeping time to beat the jet lag. She arrived at the hotel around 2 pm and, after a quick shower and change of clothes, she was ready to start exploring.

Gabrielle had bought an Insight New York City Pocket Map that she had studied on the plane and planned a few days out.

"I know it's an adventure, but some structure won't go amiss".
    She had been trying to decipher the New York street system ...

"Odd-numbered streets go west, and even-numbered streets go east. Right, ok .... And odd-numbered buildings are on the north side of the street, and even-numbered addresses are on the south. So streets run east to west, and avenues run north to south. I think I got it".

· · ·

She ventured to Time Square, then the New York Public Library on Fifth Avenue and then a little spontaneous wander for her first outing.

Everything was so new and yet so familiar. She recognised buildings and streets at almost every other turn.

Hello there, she thought as a handsome guy was walking by, going in the opposite direction.

"Talk to self; you just arrived, Gabri. Give it time".

As they crossed each other paths, the stranger smiled at her, a dazzling smile. He wasn't her usual type. She usually liked the tall, dark, handsome ones (or blonde) but definitely tall. She was 5.5ish and liked wearing heels.

He was more of an average height, a.k.a. shorter, with a soap opera-ish all American look.

"Nice shoes", he said.

Interesting pick-up line.

"Pardon?"

Gabrielle replied.

"You look like you're walking with purpose. Are you going somewhere specific?"

· · ·

She didn't want to give too much away; he was a perfect stranger after all. He could be Jack The Ripper or Ted Bunty for all she knew. And before she could answer,

"I'm on my way to the office for a meeting. Here is my card with my cell and office extension. Can I meet you for a drink later on?"

Mmmmmh ...

"Or perhaps a coffee tomorrow morning?"
   he said as she looked pensive.

Ok, that sounded more reasonable. Gabrielle was still hesitating.

"You can come into the building where I work and ask for me, and then we can go for a coffee?".
   Better. Definitely better.

"Let's say 10 am? How does that sound?".

"Sounds like a plan", she replied.

"And what is your name, lovely lady?"

· · ·

"Gabrielle".

"Nice to meet you, Gabrielle. I'll see you tomorrow. Bye".

VP OF CORPORATE FINANCE - said the business card. VP uh? Not a bad start for an adventure.

The second morning she had the American breakfast at the hotel; she wasn't quite used to having breakfast in the morning, but she thought it was better to have one considering she had planned a long day out walking—eggs, bacon, sausage and pancakes.

She had contemplated all night if to go and meet the VP.

"What have I got to lose? It's just coffee and a chat in a public space. What's the worse that can happen?".

His office was in a massive building (aren't they all) in MidTown Manhattan by the Rockefeller Center. The reception buzzed his office extension to let him know Gabrielle was there.

"You look lovely today,"
    he said. He smelled of fresh cologne and had a crisp blue striped shirt, making his eyes stand out.

. . .

"Let's go. It is only a few minutes away, right down the steps from 1 Rockefeller Plaza. There is a nice coffee bar with espressos and very nice coffee in general. You'll like it".

He was very talkative and wanted to know more about Gabrielle. Not too much, but more. The VP was making plans for the weekend. Brunch at Balthazar.

We can do this. We can do that. Plans for the two of them.

A bit presumptuous.

Mind, it was her first weekend in New York, and she quite liked the idea of having some company. The fact that she was there for a limited amount of time made it more appealing.

Probably to both of them.

Time flew quickly. He had to go back to the office, and they agreed to meet outside Balthazar. Gabrielle had plans to walk some more and had studied her map. She was so proud when someone who looked like a tourist asked her for directions.

"Success".

Everything was going so well until she reached the West Village, and then it went Pete Tong,

"What happened here?"

. . .

The familiar grid-like street system was nowhere to see. As she walked around, she stumbled on the Magnolia Bakery. She got a couple of cupcakes to see what the fuss was about.

Gabrielle tried to look for familiar landmarks and streets to get back to the hotel.

"I'd be damned if I get out the map",
    she said to herself. She could have easily reached for a taxi, but she wanted to walk. Needed to walk.

She arrived back at the hotel exhausted and went straight to bed. Day two was over by 8 pm—rock'n roll, baby.

She woke up in the morning and took the time to savour her coffee and enjoy the New York view, still not believing she was actually here.

"Time to get ready for brunch".
    That day was the beginning of her affair with the VP.

He became her chaperon with benefits. He knew how to live and have fun. The high New York life.

Their relationship grew into a whirlwind, inhibited affair.
    She felt like she was in a movie that, one day, was going to end inevitably—all more exciting for it.

· · ·

Theatres. Cinemas. Museums.

Gabrielle got to know the most famous spots in New York. And got to have sex there too.

The VP bought her a lot of gifts. Perfume. Flowers. Jewellery. Money was his "love" language. Lots of lingerie. He loved Victoria's Secrets. She had to clear a drawer just for it.

He was the perfect chaperon and was not shy in introducing her to his acquaintances.

"This is Gabrielle, my *friend* visiting from London, England", he would introduce her.

The VP took her to his place in the Hamptons too. He had a house in Cooper's Beach.

Gabrielle had heard of the Hamptons: the group of towns, and villages on the eastern end of Long Island in New York state, a popular getaway for people from New York City.

When the VP told her the Hamptons were in New York, she was perplexed. It took them about two-and-a-half hours by car to get to Westhampton, where the Hamptons start.

Two-and-half-hours!

· · ·

And to reach the end of the island's South Fork is another 50 miles east.

It's like saying Manchester is in London.

"Perspective, Gabrielle, everything is a matter of perspective", she thought.

Gabrielle could see why so many of the wealthy and famous spend their summers here: ocean breezes, white sand beaches, excellent seafood, lively parties, and the rural atmosphere of Long Island's South Fork and the more laid-back Southampton Town.

For the weekend, the VP had planned a visit to the Shinnecock Golf Club, one of the historic golfing institutions in the United States apparently.

Even though it has been renovated and expanded, its character remains substantially the same as a century ago. An accompanying member must sign in all guests;

obviously, the VP was a member. He also bought her the appropriate golf attire and briefed her on the Club's strict rules.

"Hello, are you there? Honey?"
Mr Wonderful said.

"You seem miles away. Are you ok?"

· · ·

Gabrielle was yanked back into present London.

"Yes, yes, I was just enjoying the food and lost in my thoughts",

"I hope he hasn't been talking about something important, and I missed it", she thought.

They finished their pre-theatre dinner and strolled toward the Royal Opera House around the corner. Hand in hand. Like the day they met, the electricity between was palpable. Was it too good to be true? Sometimes she doubted she deserved him / it.

They were going to see Madame Butterfly, the fascinating and heartbreaking story of words and promises carelessly spoken with inevitable consequences.

Un bel dì, vedremo
Levarsi un fil di fumo
Sull'estremo confin del mare
E poi la nave appare
Poi la nave bianca .....

The VP had taken Gabrielle to the Metropolitan to see Madame Butterfly. Because he loved Opera, better still, be seen at the Opera, the best seats of course.

· · ·

"I love this aria",
he said.

It is incredible how the same experience can differ at different times. The music transported her in and out of her body, back and forward in time.

> ....*Entra nel porto*
> *Romba il suo saluto*
> *Vedi? È venuto!*
> *Io non gli scendo incontro, io no*
> *Mi metto là sul ciglio del colle e aspetto*
> *E aspetto gran tempo*
> *E non mi pesa*
> *La lunga attesa*

Mr Wonderful looked at Gabrielle and kissed her gently on her forehead,
"Io sono qui, e non mi pesa la lunga attesa. Io ti aspetto".

SEARCHING FOR GOREN

THE NINE LIVES OF GABRIELLE: FOR
THREE SHE PLAYS - BOOK 2

Reality can be so much better than fantasy.
If you'd only let it.

PREFACE

What if we are always choosing people who don't allow intimacy?

Is it because, deep down, we don't want intimacy? Or are we afraid we'd lose ourselves entirely if we let ourselves be loved?

Committed to not committing.

"Io sono qui, e non mi pesa la lunga attesa. Io ti aspetto", said Mr Wonderful whilst looking at Gabrielle and kissing her gently on her forehead.

The singer was belting one of Madame Butterfly's most famous arias, Un bel dì, vedremo:

> *E non mi pesa*
> *La lunga attesa*
> *E uscito dalla folla cittadina*
> *Un uomo, un picciol punto*
> *S'avvia per la collina*
> *Chi sarà, chi sarà?*
> *E come sarà giunto*
> *Che dirà, che dirà?*

She smiled, not knowing what to say. Sometimes he could read her mind, and right now, she was sure he knew she had been miles away.

Madame Butterfly always had the power to take her back to the mini-sabbatical she had in New York and the performance she saw at the Metropolitan Opera in the Lincoln Center.

The auditorium combines old-world elegance with sleek contemporary, with around 3,800 seats and 245 standing-room positions. The acoustic is superb.

Grandiose.

. . .

For Gabrielle, though, the Met is just too big. Instead, she prefers the Royal Opera House in London, with 2,256 odd seats offering a far more intimate experience.

Like New York - London. The VP and Mr Wonderful.

Madame Butterfly with the VP was a show, an occasion to get dressed, socialise and be seen.

With Mr Wonderful was a moment to cherish if she could only stop being dragged back.

Is the past ever gone? Memories intruded the present moment, fantasies dropping into the continuous present of our lives.

Everything is always present. Vivid imagining sometimes feels more real than reality itself.

How easy to be confused.

The New York trip kept popping in her mind, intruding.

A last-minute decision after a long-term relationship break-up. She needed to escape, an adventure, re-group and re-think what she would do.

On her taxi ride from the airport, she felt like a mini Indiana Jones on her first-ever trip alone, non-work-related. Not visiting anybody. Nothing planned. Just her and New York. Exhilarating and scary AF.

She had decided to go for three months, longer than the usual holiday but short enough not to need a working visa.

It seemed like a good idea at the time.

By the second month there, the novelty was wearing thin without a job or friends to meet and the VP at work during the day.

Gabrielle had walked Manhattan from top to bottom and east to west. She had almost memorised every street.

Well, it certainly felt like it.

She had met the VP on her first day there, and they had been going out ever since. He had taken her to all his haunts and introduced her to all the right people (HIS right people)

—the perfect chaperon with benefits.

She was bored.

Holidays are relatively short periods that one plans. This New York trip had been unexpected, totally unplanned and without any schedule, and Gabrielle was always used to having something occupying her mind, side by side with a very active social life.

· · ·

She was so bored that she started watching television far more than she was used to back home, flicking from channel to channel (far too many).

She often settled for the Law and Order franchise, something familiar to watch, always a fan of murder mysteries and crime dramas. Gabrielle was particularly fond of Law and Order Criminal Intent and one of its characters: Detective Robert Goren, played brilliantly by character actor Vincent D'Onofrio.

Detective Goren was tall, dark and handsome, moody and incredibly perceptive in a Sherlockesque deducing manner.
    He also is totally screwed up in his relationships.

In other words: perfect and her usual type.

To pass her time, she started googling to find out where they were filming, if any filming was going on, and which actor was filming.
    She considered going too.

Reddit seemed the place to find out together with every possible D'Onofrio/Goren sighting, the two more and more intertwined in Gabrielle's mind. An intelligent and attractive hero, right here in New York. Where she was right now.

She was almost living a double life.
    By night living the sparkling NY City life with the VP.

By day searching the internet for the latest place where Goren had been seen:

- Bond St,
- Stuyvesant Town,
- Bleecker Street ...

One day, she read that he was a regular in Tompkins Square Park, Christodora House, so she walked down from MidTown and stayed there for hours.

H-O-U-R-S.

Waiting.

Nothing happened, of course, besides that she had turned into a semi-stalker.

Then, on her way back to the TownePlace, she saw him. Right at the intersection of Third Avenue and 14th Street.
   Goren was driving a big dark Range Rover.

Ok, no clue what car it was, a big one. Her heart was beating fast. She actually saw him. Live.

And, just like that, he was gone. Just like that, she had turned into an obsessed teenage stalker.

Splendid.

God knows what she thought she would do had she properly met him. Fall madly in love and move permanently to New York. Or him moving to London? She hadn't thought that far.

She was just searching for something and not finding it. She hated to admit that she was always going for emotionally or physically unavailable men.

What if she was always choosing people who don't allow intimacy? Was it because, deep down, she didn't want it?

Or was she afraid she'd lose herself entirely if she let herself be loved?
    Was SHE the one afraid?

How could she stop hooking up with emotionally unavailable people? People who can't actually love her.

And now, here she was, with Mr Wonderful.

Right here, right now, the most physically and emotionally available man she had ever met.
    Totally devoted to her.

. . .

She could see a common denominator when she looked back at her quasi-relationships that didn't work out.

Herself.

The Working-Class Millionaire who worked very hard for his money. And the more he earned, the harder he had to work to balance out his low inner worth set point.

"He is a m-i-l-l-i-o-n-a-i-r-e" his mouth filling up.
   One of the very first things he ever told her.

He was constantly trying to surpass his father, a working-class immigrant who made a fortune post-war but he never believed he could.

She never understood how an investment banker had such an aversion to money and being wealthy.

Truth be told, he had never quite adapted to his new habitat.

But, on the other hand, Gabrielle was always striving to improve, and that attitude was inconceivable to her - she had left her village behind,
   both mentally and physically.

. . .

She couldn't quite understand how one would want to remain a moth instead of becoming a butterfly.

The Stud was tall and muscular with deep green eyes, voluptuous lips, and a voracious sexual appetite.

The fact that he was several years younger than she made it even more exciting, talking about men-in-power-with younger totty in tow.

Except for this time, she was the one in power, for a change, and the man was the totty.

The thrill, coupled with the validation, was a potent aphrodisiac. And at the beginning, it was fun and exciting, but after a while, it became tedious; she wanted a proper relationship, not every weekend alone.

And even though all the signs were there, she ignored them.

He was a cancer survivor in remission who used his cancer as his Linus blanket.

Gabrielle had thought of leaving him so many times, and the sob story would come out each time.

· · ·

She had fallen for someone with so many red flags that he could have been an air traffic controller. But, giving him the benefit of the doubt, she continued to see him.

She didn't want to be the heartless cow that went him when he was down in the dumps, depressed.

Six months after they finally split, she came across a charity website and there it was: a picture of a couple who had a very successful fundraising event -

The Stud and his girlfriend.

The problem was that the fundraising event took place when they were still together. Gabrielle had been THE OTHER WOMAN.

Then came the QC. The famous QC.

Smart, attractive, with his life, totally figured out. And someone with bigger balls than hers.

But, perhaps, in insight, they were too big.

The QC was brilliant, and Gabrielle enjoyed their long debates, proud he was comfortable talking about his cases and asked her opinion.

. . .

His mind was absolutely mesmerising. His ego was equally ginormous. A man used to live life on his terms with people around him accommodating every single one of his whims.

That's how Gabriele liked it too. It was unbearable mainly because it was like looking in a mirror and not quite liking what you see.

The Champagne Socialist followed. Another mirror but, this time, not liking that much what you see. Perfection is so hard to achieve, and trying to be perfect all the time is exhausting.
Perfectionitis is a terrible disease.

Always striving, never arriving.

Gabrielle had kept looking, convinced that she'd find someone who wanted to be with her because she was *special*.

Like the Champagne Socialist: working-class, uber gifted, scholarship for Eton, EVP in one of the Big 4 consulting firms, and still suffering from Impostor Syndrome.

They were the same man. They were HER. Gabrielle was afraid of getting hurt. It was not them.
It was her.

Truly opening up to someone and having them reciprocate is an intimate bond. What if the relationship fails?

. . .

They were perfect and the safe option. Since they were guarding their emotions closely, there was a decreased risk of emotional engagement. A.K.A. getting hurt.

Gabrielle couldn't deny that the thrill of the dating chase was fun.

Wanting what you cannot have it's a never-ending, dead-end chase with intermittent positive reinforcement. Up and down. Reward and withdrawal.

Committed to not committing.

And in New York, she was living a fantasy in her head that didn't require putting in an effort to make an *actual* relationship work.

So the VP was the holiday fling and Goren, Goren, was the ultimate emotionally unavailable person, someone she "couldn't have" because he didn't actually exist.

A television character brilliantly interpreted. That's all.

And now this fantastic man was in her life, and she couldn't find any faults. He was present and engaging in a more profound, authentic and emotional way. Mr Wonderful had never made any promises that he hadn't kept. He was there, fully, completely, emotionally and physically available.

Ed egli alquanto in pena
Chiamerà, chiamerà
"Piccina, mogliettina
Olezzo di verbena"
I nomi che mi dava al suo venire
Tutto questo avverrà, te lo prometto
Tienti la tua paura
Io con sicura fede l'aspetto

As the heartbreaking song was coming to an end, a tear started rushing down her cheek.

"It's ok", he said, "it's ok .
      Io sono qui, e ti aspetto,"

AFTERWORD

Consciousness itself creates the material world. The linear passing of time in stark contrast with the seemingly random crossing of time in our consciousness.

And the stream is constant.

Everything is NOW. And memories provide a constant connection to events, places and people.

There are infinite possibilities that the world can offer at every moment .

Choose wisely.

Laura xxx

TASTING FREEDOM

THE NINE LIVES OF GABRIELLE: FOR
THREE SHE PLAYS - BOOK 3

To whomever is trying to find themselves or their dreams right now;
look within. They are right there, waiting.

PREFACE

Are you searching and never finding? The perfect place, perfect man, or woman, perfect career? Do you actually know what you are looking for in the first place?

To create what you want to have or achieve in the future implies and needs that you understand the here and.

Constantly chasing what you could have or whom you might meet means you ignore what exists all around you that already IS incredible.

Or, even worse, the incredible people who exist all around you.

Happiness and fulfilment already exist in your life, and they start with you. First and foremost.

Enjoy your life as it comes whilst working to be the best you.

The rest will take care of itself.

I t was the weekend, and Gabrielle reflected on the night out with Mr Wonderful. He had arranged dinner and Opera tickets to see Madam Butterfly, one of her favourite operas, to celebrate their meeting day.

Only a few months had passed since, and they had moved at the lighting speed. From meeting in the street to dinner/date to being in the same bubble in the last lockdown. And after that, he never left.

He seemed to remember every moment they had: their first meeting, first kiss, the first time they made love, their first weekend together. And celebrate it.

This amazing man in her life engaged in a more profound, authentic and emotional way than she had ever experienced. Fully, completely, emotionally and physically available.

Getting to know Gabrielle was like peeling an onion's multiple layers. She understood this about herself. She has had friends for over ten years who have never been to her house. Always kept something back. *Truly* opening up to anyone requires a level of intimacy she wasn't used to. And never liked. It required vulnerability.

The smell of coffee was permeating the room at the NoMad London hotel. He had thought of that too to continue the celebration into the weekend. Right in Covent Garden adjacent to the Royal Opera House, in the Bow Street Magistrates' Court Building. Splendid.

. . .

"Good morning, darling", he said, just back from the fitness centre. "I'm going in the shower. Want to join me?"

Dejavu.

"Obviously", she replied.

"How are you this morning?" Mr Wonderful enquired. His voice had an underlying worrying tone. Gabrielle had to do something to reassure him. Her mind wandered off and on all evening.

London - New York -London- New York. A round-the-world trip in one single evening. Better still, a round-the-world trip in her memories and back.

She felt so guilty.

New York had been an essential step in her life. The action that ultimately got her here today.

Becoming the woman she was today, albeit still a work in progress.

. . .

Three months were, she did not have the single-vision focus of her career but allowed herself to grow. In whichever direction. A last-minute decision to take a New York trip after a long-term relationship breakup turned out to be one of her best decisions to date. Besides giving her phone number to Mr Wonderful.

"Can I have your number?"
    he said, and then he called her straight away.

"You can't be missing me already; I'm still here,"
    Gabrielle told him, teasing.

"I just want to make sure I have the right number. And you now have mine too",
    grinning from side to side.
    "Are you sure I cannot convince you to have dinner with me tonight?".

That was for sure her best decision. But New York was a close second.

Three months in a different city, another country, led to further thinking. But, you take yourself wherever you go, and Gabrielle did just that initially and started a brief affair post-arrival that lasted almost two months.

But eventually, she came to her senses. She decided to REALLY explore the city. Not just the usual suspects like

Central Park, the Statue of Liberty or the Empire State Building but also, for example, the small breakfast cafe around the corner that served the biggest breakfast she had ever seen.

She walked in alone. Sat down with no distractions or barriers and ordered. What seemed like the smallest item on the menu.

"A cheese and ham omelette, please".

After a short time, the most humongous plate of food arrived at her table.

"Excuse me," she said. "I'm sorry, I think this is the wrong order. I asked for a cheese and ham omelette?"

"That's right," the server said. "That's it, honey".

The plate was overflowing. God knows how many eggs were used; probably a whole battery of hens was at work here. And there were chips, bread slices, and so on.

 Gabrielle struggled to finish the omelette itself and left all the "garnish" behind.

"What's wrong, honey?"

the server looked worried.

"Was there something wrong with the food? You left the majority behind ... Do you want to take it away?"

"Good Lord, no", Gabrielle was thinking. "Far more carbs than I have ever seen in my life".

"I wasn't that hungry; it was delicious, thank you,"
she said aloud and made sure she left a generous tip behind.

She also learned to wander the various neighbourhoods; slow and purposeful walks to get to know the area, even better, people. She was not afraid to ask questions and be seen as the tourist that she actually was. Or someone just learning. Shocking.

She stopped seeing the VP around her second month in New York and started to go out. Alone. Dinners. Theatres.

She even booked herself in a writers' conference, something she had always wanted to do.

The VP didn't take it very well. Not that he ever wanted to pursue a long-distance relationship, but he was at least counting on keeping the relationship going until at least she was departing.

. . .

At the writers' conference, she met many people, most Americans, a mix of professional, semi-professional, amateurs and wanna-be writers. All extraordinarily nice and friendly. All were extremely surprised but supportive of her first trip alone.

"You are here alone?"

"Yes, I am. I am not visiting anybody. And I had nothing planned, nowhere specific to go when I arrived" proud moment.

Gabrielle felt great about herself now. Even better knowing that everyone recognised she had been courageous. They didn't realise that the scariest part of her trip had been walking into a restaurant for dinner alone. For the first time ever.

Much harder than travelling across the world. The inner battles are always the hardest and the most satisfying when you win.

And the second most challenging thing was the realisation that the men she had dated, their red flags, were her red flags. They just carried them around for her. And she had decided it was time to put them down, once and for all.

All the men she dated were the same man.
    They were HER.

. . .

They were exactly right for her each time because they were safe and presented no real risk of ultimately getting hurt.

Gabrielle realised she had been committed to not committing.
  "That's a commitment for you," she thought, smiling.

Slowly but surely, in the same New York where she lived the fantasy of pursuing Detective Goren, she slowly broke her shackles.

"I'm good darling, Terrific. Never better,"
  she said, smiling. "I think I owe you an apology".

"No, you don't. I just want to know you are ok, that we are ok".

"Absolutely", she said." So, let's have that shower and then a chat?"

"It's not one of those 'We need to talk' moments, right?"
  Mr Wonderful asked.

"No, no, no …."

"Vicar of Dibley?" he asked, smiling.

. . .

"No, no, YES ... no", she replied, smiling.

After a long, steamy shower, they went for a walk and just like that, Gabrielle started talking.

For the first time, really talking: she told him about New York, the why, the when and the how. She told him everything.

Ok, not E-V-E-R-Y-T-H-I-N-G.

She omitted the chasing Vincent D'Onofrio/Goren around NYC like a crazy person.

"This onion needs to keep some layers,"
    she thought. At least for now.

And as their day was ending, her shackles were falling even more, and Gabrielle was finally tasting freedom.

Freedom is an elusive concept.
Some men hold themselves prisoner even when they have the
power to do as they please and go where they choose, while
others are free in their hearts, even as shackles restrain them.

-- Brian Herbert

AFTERWORD

Vulnerability is where courage and fear meet. It is awkward and scary, but it is also freedom and liberation.

Being uniquely you: embracing your imperfections and daring to be vulnerable, engaging fully and openly with the world around you, being open despite knowing it might hurt you, feeling love, belonging and joy.

It feels a bit like going out there without makeup, with no armour hoping the real you isn't too disappointing. And still feeling worthy.

Ouch! I know, it sound scary.

But realise that you ARE worthy. Right here, right now. Perfectly imperfect and absolutely fabulous.

Laura xxx

DISCLAIMER

The Nine Lives of Gabrielle: For Three She Plays is a work of fiction.

Although its form is that of an autobiography, it is not one.

With the exception of public places, any resemblance to persons living or dead is coincidental. Space and time have been rearranged to suit the convenience of the book, memory has its own story to tell.

The opinions expressed are those of the characters and should not be confused with the author's.

AUTHOR'S NOTE

Thank you so much for buying and reading *The Nine Lives of Gabrielle: For Three She Plays,* a collection of three short stories.

If enjoyed these novellas a review would be much appreciated as it helps other readers discover the story. Thanks.

If you sign up for my newsletter you'll be notified of giveaways, new releases and receive personal updates from behind the scenes of my business and books.

Go to www.thepeoplealchemist.com to get started.

Places in the book

I have set the story in real places in London and New York - find out more about them or perhaps, go and visit:

- Balthazar, London
- Balthazar, New York
- Blue Bottle Coffee
- Central Park

- Covent Garden
- Empire State Building
- Magnolia Bakery
- NoMad London
- Rockefeller Center
- Royal Opera House, London
- The New York Public Library
- The Metropolitan Opera, New York
- The Shinnecock Golf Club
- The Statue of Liberty
- Times Square
- TownePlace Suites, Manhattan/Times Square
- NYC West Village

Bibliography

I read a lot of books as part of my research. Some of them together with other references include:

Psycho-Cybernetics - **Maxwell Maltz**
The Complete Reader - **Neville Goddard**

The Vicar of Dibley - British sitcom starring Dawn French as the Vicar of the rural parish of Dibley, It made its debut in 1994.

The **"Bermondsey Goes Balearic"** article in the late 1987 by Paul Oakenfold for Terry Farley and Pete Heller's Boys Own fanzine (*it's all gone Pete Tong*).

Madama Butterfly is an opera in three acts by Giacomo Puccini, with an Italian libretto by Luigi Illica and Giuseppe Giacosa, premiered at La Scala, in Milan in 1904.

Printed in Great Britain
by Amazon

80721309R00051